Saffron
the Yellow
Fairy

by Daisy Meadows

illustrated by Georgie Ripper

Join the Rainbow Magic Reading Challenge!

Read the story and collect your fairy points to climb the
Reading Rainbow at the back of the book.

This book is worth 5 points.

The Fairyland Palace
Maze
Forest
Orchard
Black Pot
Meadow
Tower
Beach
Rockpools
Rainspell Island

Cold winds blow and thick ice form,
I conjure up this fairy storm.
To seven corners of the mortal world
the Rainbow Fairies will be hurled!

I curse every part of Fairyland,
with a frosty wave of my icy hand.
For now and always, from this fateful day,
Fairyland will be cold and grey!

Ruby and Amber have been rescued.
Now it's time to search for
Saffron the Yellow Fairy

Contents

A Very Fierce Bee

"Over here, Kirsty!" called Rachel
Walker. Kirsty ran down one of the
emerald green fields that covered this
part of Rainspell Island. Buttercups and
daisies dotted the grass.

"Don't go too far!" Kirsty's mum called.
She and Kirsty's dad were climbing over
a stile at the top of the field.

Kirsty caught up with her friend. "What have you found, Rachel? Is it another Rainbow Fairy?" she asked hopefully.

"I don't know." Rachel was standing on the bank of a rippling stream. "I thought I heard something."

Kirsty's face lit up. "Maybe there's a fairy in the stream?"

Rachel nodded. She knelt down on the soft grass and put her ear close to the water.

Kirsty crouched down too, and listened really hard.

The sun glittered on the water as it splashed over big, shiny pebbles. Tiny rainbows flashed and sparkled – red, orange, yellow, green, blue, indigo, and violet.

And then they heard a tiny bubbling voice. "Follow me..." it gurgled. "Follow me..."

"Oh!" Rachel gasped. "Did you hear that?"

"Yes," said Kirsty, her eyes wide. "It must be a *magic* stream!"

Rachel felt her heart beat fast. "Maybe the stream will lead us to the Yellow Fairy," she said.

Rachel and Kirsty had a special secret. They had promised the King and Queen of Fairyland they would find the lost Rainbow Fairies. Jack Frost's spell had hidden the Rainbow Fairies on Rainspell Island. Fairyland would be cold and grey until all seven fairies had been found and returned to their home.

Silver fish darted in and out of the bright green weed at the bottom of the stream. "Follow us, follow us..." they whispered in tinkling voices.

Rachel and Kirsty smiled at each other. Titania, the Fairy Queen, had said that the magic would find them!

Kirsty's parents had stopped to admire the stream too. "Which way now?" asked Mr Tate. "You two seem to know where you're going."

"Let's go this way," Kirsty said, pointing along the bank.

A brilliant blue kingfisher flew up from its perch on a twig. Butterflies as bright as jewels fluttered amongst the reeds.

"Everything on Rainspell Island is so beautiful," said Kirsty's mum. "I'm glad we still have five days of holiday left!"

Yes, Rachel thought, and five Rainbow Fairies still to find: Saffron, Fern, Sky, Izzy – and Heather!

Ruby the Red Fairy and Amber the Orange Fairy were already safe in the pot-at-the-end-of-the-rainbow.

The girls ran on ahead of Mr and Mrs Tate. As they followed the bubbling stream, the sun went behind a big, dark cloud.

A chilly breeze ruffled Kirsty's hair. She saw that some of the leaves on the trees were turning brown, even though it wasn't autumn. "It looks like Jack Frost's goblins are still around," she warned Rachel.

"I know." Rachel gave a shiver. "Horrible things! They'll do anything to stop the Rainbow Fairies getting back to Fairyland."

The two friends stared anxiously up at the sky. But then the sun came out again. They smiled with relief.

The stream ran through a meadow covered with green clover. A herd of black and white cows were grazing at the water's edge. They looked up with their huge, brown eyes.

"Aren't they lovely?" Kirsty said.

Suddenly the cows tossed their heads and ran off towards the other end of the field.

Rachel and Kirsty looked at each other in surprise. What was going on?

There was a loud buzzing noise.

A small angry shape came whizzing through the air, straight towards them! Rachel almost jumped out of her skin. "It's a bee!" she gasped.

"Run!" Kirsty cried. The cows had got the right idea! Rachel tore through the meadow with Kirsty beside her, their feet pounding the grass.

"Keep running, girls," called Mr Tate, catching up with them. "That bee seems to be following us!"

Rachel glanced back. The bee was huge, bigger than any bee she'd ever seen.

"In here, quick!" Mrs Tate called
from the side of the field. She pulled
open a wooden gate.

They all ran through it, then stopped
to get their breath.

"I wonder who lives here?" Kirsty
panted. They were in a beautiful
garden. A path led up to a thatched
cottage with yellow roses around the
door.

Just then, a very strange creature came out from behind some trees. It looked like an alien from outer space!

"Oh!" Rachel and Kirsty gasped.

The creature lifted its gloved hands and removed its white helmet to reveal...an old lady! She smiled at them. "Sorry if I startled you," she said. "I do look a bit strange in my beekeeper's suit."

Rachel sighed in relief. It wasn't a space alien after all!

"I'm Mrs Merry," the old lady went on.

"Hello," Rachel said. "I'm Rachel. This is my friend, Kirsty."

"And this is my mum and dad," Kirsty added.

Mr and Mrs Tate greeted Mrs Merry.

Then Mr Tate ducked as the huge bee zoomed past his ear.

"Watch out!" he said.

"Oh, it's that hiveless queen again," said Mrs Merry. She flapped her hand at the bee. "Go on, shoo!" Rachel watched it swoop over a low hedge and disappear.

"Why did the bee chase us?" Kirsty asked.

"I don't think she was chasing you, my dear," said Mrs Merry. "She was just heading this way because she's looking for a hive of her own. But all of mine already have queens."

"Well, thank goodness she's gone now!" said Mrs Tate.

"Since you're here, would you like to try some of my honey?" Mrs Merry asked. Her blue eyes sparkled merrily.

"Oh, yes please," said Rachel.

The others nodded, and they followed Mrs Merry across the lawn to a table covered with rows of jars.

21

Each jar was filled with rich golden honey. Dappled sunlight danced over the jars, making the honey glow.

"Here you are," said Mrs Merry, spooning some honey on to a pretty, yellow plate.

"Thank you," Rachel said politely. She dipped her finger into the little pool of honey and popped it into her mouth. The honey was the most delicious she had ever tasted – sweet and smooth.

Then she felt it begin to tingle on her tongue. She looked across at Kirsty. "It tastes all fizzy!" she whispered.

Kirsty dipped her finger into the honey too. "And look!" she said.

Rachel saw that the honey was sparkling with a thousand tiny, gold lights. She grabbed Kirsty's arm. "Do you think this means—"

"Yes," said Kirsty. Her eyes were shining. "Another Rainbow Fairy must be nearby!"

The Magic Hive

"We have to find out where this honey came from!" Rachel said excitedly.

"Yes," Kirsty agreed. "Mum? Can we stay here a bit longer, please?"

"As long as it's OK with Mrs Merry," Kirsty's mum replied.

Mrs Merry beamed. "Of course they can stay," she said kindly.

Mr and Mrs Tate decided to carry on with their walk. "Make sure you come back to Dolphin Cottage by lunchtime," Kirsty's mum said.

"We will," Kirsty promised.

"Come along then, girls." Mrs Merry set off across the smooth, green lawn.

Rachel and Kirsty followed her down the garden to some old and twisted apple trees. Six wooden hives stood underneath.

Kirsty stared at the row of hives. "Which one did the honey we tasted come from?" she asked.

Mrs Merry looked pleased. "Did you enjoy it? The honey from that hive tastes especially good at the moment."

Rachel and Kirsty grinned at each other.

"I think we might know why," Rachel whispered to Kirsty.

"Yes," Kirsty agreed. "It could be fairy honey!"

"That's the one," Mrs Merry said proudly, pointing to the very bottom of the garden. One hive stood there all alone, beneath the biggest apple tree.

As they drew nearer to the hive, a sleepy buzzing sound drifted up into the air. "The bees in this hive are very peaceful nowadays," said Mrs Merry. "I've never known them to be so happy."

"Can we get a bit closer?" Rachel asked eagerly. She couldn't wait to find out if the hive held a magical secret!

Mrs Merry looked thoughtful. "I think it's safe, with the bees so quiet," she decided. "But you had better wear a hood like mine, just in case."

She went into a nearby shed and brought out two beekeepers' hoods. "Here you are."

Rachel and Kirsty pulled the hoods over their heads. It was a bit dark and stuffy inside but they could see out of the fine netting.

They moved closer to the hive. The soft buzzing sounded almost like music.

"We need to open it and have a look," Kirsty whispered to Rachel.

Rachel nodded.

But they couldn't start searching for the Yellow Fairy with Mrs Merry there. Ruby had warned them that no grown-ups should see the fairies.

Suddenly Kirsty had an idea. "Mrs Merry, could I have a drink of water, please?" she asked.

"Of course you can, dear," Mrs Merry said. She went off towards the cottage.

The girls waited until Mrs Merry disappeared inside.

"Quick!" Kirsty spun round. "Let's open the hive."

Rachel grasped one end of the lid. Kirsty took hold of the other end. They pulled hard and it slowly came loose with a squeaky sound. Strings of golden honey stretched down from the lid.

"Watch out. It's very sticky," Rachel
said.

The girls bent down and laid the
heavy wooden top carefully on the
ground. Kirsty wiped her fingers on the
grass.

"Look!" Rachel whispered as she
stood up.

Kirsty turned to see, and gasped.

A shower of sparkling gold dust shot up out of the hive. It hung in a soft cloud, shimmering and dancing in the sunlight. Fairy dust!

Rachel leaned over and peered down into the hive. A tiny girl was sitting cross-legged on a piece of honeycomb, in the middle of a golden sea of honey.

A bee lay with its head in her lap while she combed its silky hair. Several other bees were waiting their turn, buzzing gently.

"Oh, Kirsty," Rachel whispered. "We've found another Rainbow Fairy!"

Bee Friends

Rachel and Kirsty took off their hoods
and stared down into the hive in delight.

The fairy had bright yellow hair.
She wore a necklace of golden
raindrops around her neck and sparkly
golden bracelets on both wrists. Her
bright yellow T-shirt and shorts were
the colour of buttercups. Her delicate

35

wings glistened with a thousand
shimmering rainbows.

"Oh, thank you for finding me!" the
fairy said in a tinkling voice. "I'm
Saffron the Yellow Fairy."

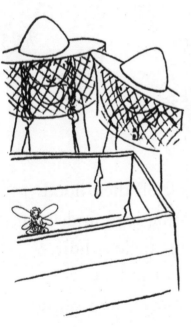

"I'm Rachel,"
said Rachel.
"And I'm Kirsty,"
said Kirsty.
"We've met two
of your sisters
already – Ruby
and Amber."
Saffron beamed
happily.
"You've found
Ruby and Amber?"
She stood up, gently
pushing the bee away.

"Yes. They're safe in the pot-at-the-
end-of-the-rainbow," Rachel said.

Saffron clapped her tiny hands. "I
can't *wait* to see them again." Suddenly
she looked worried. "Have you seen
any of Jack Frost's goblins near here?"
she asked.

"No, not here," Kirsty said. "But
there were some by the pot yesterday."

"We hid in a bush until they went
away," Rachel explained.

"Goblins are scary," Saffron said in a trembling voice. "I've been safe from them here in the hive, with my friends the bees." Rachel felt very sorry for Saffron. "It's all right. King Oberon sent one of his frog footmen to look after you and your sisters." Saffron cheered up. "I've been really worried about finding my sisters. Jack Frost's magic is so cold and strong." "It won't be long now," Kirsty said. "We are going to find Fern, Sky, Izzy, and Heather too, aren't we, Rachel?" "Yes. We promised," Rachel agreed.

"Oh, thank you!" Saffron said. She
threw out her arms and gave a shake
of her sparkling wings.

Fairy dust rose into the air and drifted
down around Rachel and Kirsty. Where
it landed, bright yellow butterflies
appeared, with tiny fluttering wings.

A large bee crawled from one of the
waxy openings in the honeycomb next
to Saffron.

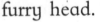

"This is my best friend, Queenie," said Saffron. She put her arms round the bee's neck and kissed the top of her furry head.

Queenie buzzed softly.

"She says hello," said Saffron.

"Hello, Queenie," Kirsty and Rachel said together.

Saffron picked up her tiny comb and began to comb Queenie's shiny hair. Another bee buzzed crossly.

"Don't worry, Petal, I'll comb your hair next," Saffron said.

Rachel and Kirsty looked at each other in dismay.

"What if Saffron wants to stay with Queenie and the other bees?" Kirsty whispered.

"Saffron, you have to come with us!" Rachel burst out. "Or Fairyland will never get its colours back! It will take all of the Rainbow sisters to undo his spell."

Forgetful Fairy

"Yes, of course! We have to break Jack Frost's spell!" Saffron cried. She jumped to her feet and picked up her wand.

Suddenly an icy wind sprung up. Something crunched under Kirsty's feet. The grass was covered with frost!

Rachel shivered as something soft and cold brushed against her cheek.

A snowflake in summer? "What's happening?" she cried.

"Jack Frost's goblins must be near," Kirsty said, worriedly.

Saffron's tiny teeth chattered with cold. "Oh, no! If they find me, they will stop me getting back to Fairyland!"

Kirsty looked at Rachel in alarm. "Quick, we must go!"

Rachel leaned down and lifted the fairy out of the hive.

Saffron's golden hair dripped with honey.

"Oh dear, you're really sticky," Rachel said.

Just then Kirsty spotted Mrs Merry coming out of her cottage.

"I'd forgotten about asking for a drink," Kirsty said. "What are we going to do?"

Rachel thought for a moment, then popped the fairy into the pocket of her shorts.

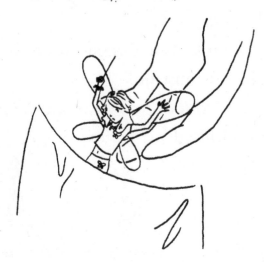

Saffron gave a cry of dismay. "Hey! It's dark in here!" she complained.

"Sorry," Rachel whispered. "I'll get you out again in a minute."

Suddenly Kirsty noticed the open hive. "We have to put the top back on!" she said.

She bent down and grasped the lid. Rachel helped lift it and they quickly put it back, just as Mrs Merry came through the trees.

"Here's your drink, dear," said Mrs Merry, holding out a glass to Kirsty. She had taken off her strange suit, and in her other hand she was carrying a shopping basket.

"Thank you very much," Kirsty said, taking the glass.

"Now, you girls stay as long as you like," said Mrs Merry. "I've just remembered I must go and buy some fish for my cat."

Rachel watched the old lady go towards the garden gate. Then she slipped her hand into her pocket.

"You can come out now," she said to
Saffron, lifting her out.

The fairy was covered with grey fluff
from Rachel's pocket. "Achoo!" she
sneezed. She brushed crossly at the bits
of sticky fluff clinging to her wings.
"I'm all clogged up!" she wailed. "I
won't be able to fly."

"We need to clean you up," Rachel
said. "But we'll have to be quick, in
case the goblins find us."

Kirsty looked round and spotted a stone bird bath filled with clear water. "Over there." She pointed.

"Just what we need," Rachel agreed. She carried Saffron over to the bird bath.

Saffron fluttered on to the edge of the bath, put down her wand, and dived in.

Splash!

The water fizzed and turned bright yellow. Lemony-smelling drops shot everywhere.

Saffron swam two circles, then she was sparkling clean. She zoomed up into the air to dry. Misty yellow trails appeared as she whooshed about. "That's better!" she cried.

She hovered in front of Kirsty. Her wings flashed like gold in the sun. Then she swooped on to Rachel's shoulder. "Come on, let's go to the pot-at-the-end-of-the-rainbow!"

Rachel nodded. She wanted to leave the garden before the goblins got there.

"Goodbye, Queenie!" Saffron called, waving to her friend.

Queenie looked out of the entrance to the hive. She seemed a bit sad that Saffron was going. Her feelers drooped as she waved a tiny leg and buzzed goodbye.

Saffron sat cross-legged on Rachel's
shoulder as they headed for the woods.
Suddenly she gave a cry and flew up
into the air. "Oh, no!" she gasped.
"I've left my wand beside the bird bath!"

Rachel looked at Kirsty in dismay.
"We'll have to go back," she said.

"Yes," Kirsty agreed. "We can't leave
a fairy wand lying about for the
goblins to find."

"Oh, dear... Oh, dear..." Saffron zipped back and forth, wringing her hands as they went back along the path.

Rachel paused at the gate and looked into the garden. There was no sign of any goblins.

Kirsty and Rachel ran through the apple trees, straight to Queenie's hive. Saffron fluttered just above them.

Suddenly an icy blast made them all shiver. They gazed around in alarm. Icicles now hung from the apple trees, and the whole lawn was white and crunchy with frost. The goblins had arrived! And they'd brought winter to the lovely garden.

Saffron gave a cry of horror.

An ugly, hook-nosed goblin jumped up on top of Queenie's hive. His bulging eyes gleamed, and in his hand he was holding Saffron's wand!

Well Done, Queenie

"Give me back my wand!"
Saffron demanded.

"Come and get it!"
yelled the goblin rudely.
He leaped off the hive and
ran towards the garden gate.

Kirsty gasped as another goblin
jumped down from the apple tree. *Splat!*

He landed on the frosty grass and set off at a run.

"Catch!" The goblin threw the wand to his friend. It flew through the air, shooting out yellow sparks.

The other goblin reached up and caught the wand. "Hee, hee. Got it!"

"Oh, no!" Saffron gasped.

Just then, Queenie flew out of the hive with a loud buzz. All the other bees swarmed behind her in a noisy cloud.

Rachel watched, her eyes very wide. With Queenie in the lead, the bees formed into an arrow shape and surged after the goblins.

"Be careful, Queenie!" pleaded Saffron.

"Get away!" The goblin shook Saffron's wand at Queenie.

More bright yellow sparks shot out of the wand. One of the sparks hit Queenie's wing. Queenie wobbled in mid-air. Then she buzzed crossly and flew at the goblin again.

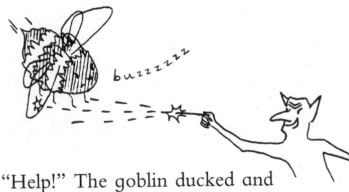

buzzzzz

"Help!" The goblin ducked and dropped the wand.

"Butterfingers!" grumbled the other goblin, scooping it up.

"They're getting away!" Kirsty said in dismay.

Queenie and her bees rose into the air again.

"No, they're not!" Rachel cried

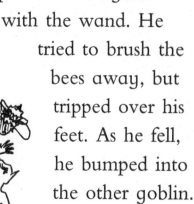

excitedly. The bees shot across the garden and the goblins disappeared under an angry, black cloud.

"Get off me!" spluttered the goblin

with the wand. He tried to brush the bees away, but tripped over his feet. As he fell, he bumped into the other goblin.

They tumbled over in a heap, dropping the wand on to the grass.

"That was your fault!" complained one of the goblins.

"No, it wasn't!" snapped the other one.

Queenie zoomed over and picked up the wand in her tiny, black feet.

She carried it straight to Saffron, who was standing on Rachel's hand. With a little buzz, Queenie landed next to Saffron.

Saffron took her wand from Queenie and carefully waved it in the air. A fountain of glittering dust and fluttering butterflies sparkled around them.

"My wand is all right!" Saffron cried joyfully.

"Look! The goblins are going," Kirsty said.

The bees had chased the goblins to the end of the garden. Still arguing, they ran across the fields.

As the grumbling voices faded away, the icy wind dropped. The sun shone warmly again and the frost melted. The bees streamed back and flew around Rachel and Kirsty, buzzing softly.

"Thank you, Queenie!" Saffron's eyes sparkled as she hugged her friend.

Suddenly Queenie wobbled and tipped sideways.

Rachel cupped her hands, worried that Queenie would roll off. "I think she might be hurt," she said. Saffron knelt down and looked closely at Queenie. "Oh, no! She's torn her wing!" she gasped.

"It must have happened when she fought the goblin," Rachel said.

"Can you mend Queenie's wing with magic?" Kirsty asked Saffron.

Saffron shook her head. "Not on my own. But Amber or Ruby might be able to help me. We must take Queenie to the pot-at-the-end-of-the-rainbow at once!"

Fairy Repairs

Rachel and Kirsty hurried across the
fields and into the woods. Rachel
carefully held Queenie in her cupped
hands, while Saffron flew behind them,
her rainbow-coloured wings shimmering
in the sun.

"There's the willow tree where the
pot is hidden," Kirsty said. She went

over and parted the branches, which
hung right down to the ground. The
black pot lay on its side in the grass.
A large, green frog hopped out from
behind it.

"Bertram!" Saffron flew down and
hugged him. "I'm so glad you're here!"

Bertram bowed his head. "It's a
pleasure, Miss Saffron,"
he said. "Miss Ruby
and Miss Amber
will be delighted
to see you."

Suddenly a shower
of red and orange
fairy dust shot up out
of the pot, followed
by Ruby and Amber.

"Saffron!" Ruby shouted.
"It really is you!"
"It's good to have
you back," Amber
called happily.
Kirsty and Rachel
smiled as the fairies
hugged and kissed each other.

The air around them fizzed with red
flowers, orange bubbles and tiny,
yellow butterflies.

Ruby flew on to Kirsty's shoulder.
"Thank you, Rachel and Kirsty," she
said. "Now three of us are safe." Then
she spotted Queenie sitting on Rachel's
hand. "Who is this?" she asked.

"This is my friend, Queenie," Saffron explained. "She helped me get my wand back after the goblins stole it."

"Goblins?" Ruby gave a shudder. "You were very brave to fight them." She flew down and stroked Queenie's head.

"One of the goblins used my wand to hurt Queenie's wing. Can you help her?" Saffron asked her sisters.

Amber thought hard. "I could mend Queenie's wing if I had a fairy needle and thread," she said. Then she looked sad. "But I don't have any here on the island."

Then Rachel remembered something. "Kirsty! What about the magic bags that the Fairy Queen gave us?"

"Oh, yes," Kirsty said. She reached into her pocket and took out her bag. It was glowing with a soft, silver light.

When she opened it a cloud of glitter shot up into the air. Kirsty slipped her hand into the bag. "There's something here."

She drew out a tiny, shining needle, threaded with fine spider silk. She held it out to Amber.

"Perfect!" Amber said. She flew on to Rachel's hand.

Saffron stroked Queenie's black and
yellow head. "Don't worry," she said.
"It's fairy magic, so it won't hurt."

Kirsty watched as Amber carefully
wove the needle in and out of the tear.
The row of stitches glowed like tiny
silver dots.

"Look, they're starting to fade,"
Rachel said.

"Yes," said Amber. "When you can't
see them any more, the wing is
mended."

Queenie buzzed softly. She lifted her head and flapped her wings. Then she zoomed into the air. Her wing was as good as new! She swooped down and landed next to Amber. Bowing her head, she rubbed her feelers against the fairy's hand. "You have been such a good friend to Saffron, you must stay with us," said Amber, hugging the bee. "Yes!" Ruby agreed. "Please come and live with us in the pot."

Queenie flew over to Saffron and buzzed in her ear.

"She says she would love to," said Saffron. "There is a hiveless queen in Mrs Merry's garden who will take care of her bees. Come on, Queenie. Let's look at our new home."

"Let's have a look too," Kirsty said. Rachel crouched down beside her in the grass. They watched the fairy sisters and the queen bee go into the pot.

Saffron beamed when she saw all the tiny furniture. She sat down on a soft, mossy cushion. "This is just like our home in Fairyland," she said. Then her face fell.

"But what about our sisters? They are still trapped on the island!"

"Don't worry," Kirsty said. "We'll find them soon."

"Yes, we will," Rachel agreed, jumping up. She looked at her watch. "It's nearly lunchtime. We have to go. Goodbye, we'll see you again soon."

The fairies looked up and waved. "Goodbye! Goodbye!" Queenie waved a tiny leg and buzzed.

Bertram, the frog footman, followed
them out from under the willow tree.
"Ruby, Amber and Saffron will be safe
here with me," he said. "But you must
take care when you go looking for the
others. Watch out for goblins!"

"We will," Rachel promised.

Kirsty looked back at the pot-at-the-
end-of-the-rainbow. "Nothing will stop
us finding the other Rainbow Fairies!"
she said firmly.

Now it's time for Rachel and Kirsty to help...

Fern the Green Fairy

Read on for a sneak peek...

"Oh!" Rachel Walker gasped in delight, as she gazed around her. "What a perfect place for a picnic!"

"It's a secret garden," Kirsty Tate said, her eyes shining.

They were standing in a large garden. It looked as if nobody else had been there for a long time. Pink and white roses grew all around the tree trunks, filling the air with sweet perfume. White marble statues stood here and there, half hidden by trailing, green ivy. And right in the middle of the garden was a crumbling stone tower.

"There was a castle here once called Moonspinner Castle," Mr Walker said, looking at his guidebook. "But now all that's left is the tower."

Rachel and Kirsty stared up at the ruined tower. The yellow stones glowed warmly in the sunshine...

Read Fern the Green Fairy to find out what adventures are in store for Kirsty and Rachel!

RAINBOW magic

Calling all parents, carers and teachers!
The Rainbow Magic fairies are here to help
your child enter the magical world of reading.
Whatever reading stage they are at, there's
a Rainbow Magic book for everyone!
Here is Lydia the Reading Fairy's guide to
supporting your child's journey at all levels.

Starting Out

Our Rainbow Magic Beginner Readers are perfect for first-time readers who are just beginning to develop reading skills and confidence. Approved by teachers, they contain a full range of educational levelling, as well as lively full-colour illustrations.

Developing Readers

Rainbow Magic Early Readers contain longer stories and wider vocabulary for building stamina and growing confidence. These are adaptations of our most popular Rainbow Magic stories, specially developed for younger readers in conjunction with an Early Years reading consultant, with full-colour illustrations.

Going Solo

The Rainbow Magic chapter books - a mixture of series and one-off specials - contain accessible writing to encourage your child to venture into reading independently. These highly collectible and much-loved magical stories inspire a love of reading to last a lifetime.

www.rainbowmagicbooks.co.uk

"Rainbow Magic got my daughter reading chapter books. Great sparkly covers, cute fairies and traditional stories full of magic that she found impossible to put down" - Mother of Edie (6 years)

"Florence LOVES the Rainbow Magic books. She really enjoys reading now" - Mother of Florence (6 years)

The Rainbow Magic Reading Challenge

Well done, fairy friend – you have completed the book!
This book was worth 5 points.

See how far you have climbed on the
Reading Rainbow opposite.

The more books you read, the more points you will get,
and the closer you will be to becoming a Fairy Princess!

How to get your Reading Rainbow
1. Cut out the coin below
2. Go to the Rainbow Magic website
3. Download and print out your poster
4. Add your coin and climb up the Reading Rainbow!

There's all this and lots more at
www.rainbowmagicbooks.co.uk

You'll find activities, competitions, stories, a special
newsletter and complete profiles of all the
Rainbow Magic fairies. Find a fairy with your name!